FACE CHALLENGES,

ESCAPE

SOLVE PUZZLES,

BOOK

AND ESCAPE THE BOOK!

Mystery Island

Published in French under the title *Escape book – L'Île aux mystères*
© 2019 by 404 éditions, an imprint of Édi8, Paris, France
Text © 2019 by Stéphane Anquetil, Illustration © 2019 by Marcel Pixel

Andrews McMeel Publishing
a division of Andrews McMeel Universal
1130 Walnut Street, Kansas City, Missouri 64106
www.andrewsmcmeel.com

20 21 22 23 24 SDB 10 9 8 7 6 5 4 3 2 1

ISBN: 978-1-5248-6140-7 hardback
978-1-5248-5591-8 paperback

Library of Congress Control Number: 2020930840

Made by:
King Yip (Dongguan) Printing & Packaging Factory Ltd.
Address and location of manufacturer:
Daning Administrative District, Humen Town
Dongguan Guangdong, China 523930
1st printing—6/29/20

ATTENTION: SCHOOLS AND BUSINESSES
Andrews McMeel books are available at quantity discounts with
bulk purchase for educational, business, or sales promotional use.
For information, please e-mail the Andrews McMeel Publishing
Special Sales Department: specialsales@amuniversal.com.

FACE CHALLENGES, SOLVE PUZZLES, AND ESCAPE THE BOOK!

Mystery Island

STÉPHANE ANQUETIL

Andrews McMeel
PUBLISHING®

*Y*ou are stranded on a very mysterious island, young pirate! You'd better find a way out of here quickly, before the volcano erupts!

You awake in a smoky cave. Luckily, your parrot, Harry, is there to help you.

Go explore, find objects, solve puzzles, and escape danger. . . . Will you be able to escape in time, make some allies, and maybe even bring back treasure?

Rules of the Game

To get from place to place, you have a map that shows you the main locations on the island, using multiples of 10.

Careful! You have to follow the paths on the map rather than following the order of the numbers.

When you're at **20**, for example, you can go to **30**, **60**, or **70**.

Some places are well hidden, and the paths there are represented by dotted lines. To get there, you'll have to overcome obstacles by using specific objects and your brain power.

You'll find these objects over the course of your adventure. They'll be in **red**, such as a **rope**. Each time you find an object, make a note of it in your inventory to help you remember what you have.

When you're in a specific place where you want to use an object, you can combine it with something else. All the possible combinations are at the back of the book in **A2**. You can also find them on the inside front cover of this book.

How do these combinations work? Good question. In the tables, you'll find some numbers. Once you decide what you want to combine, go to the numbered sections in the book listed beneath them.

You'll find that some objects can even be paired in a combination. For example, with a **grappling hook** and a **rope**, you could have these options.

Rope	Grappling & Rope	Grappling Hook
220	221	222

To use the rope, you would go to **220**. To use the grappling hook and the rope together, you would go to **221**. To use the grappling hook on its own, you would go to **222**. Go ahead and read these sections to practice.

Warning! **If you don't have an object in your inventory or it's not given as an option in your combination table, you can't use it.**

In this adventure, you have a parrot, Harry, with you. He gives you advice throughout this book. But he is an unpredictable creature, and his advice can be cryptic.

This book is illustrated. For some puzzles, there are clues hidden in the pictures, so pay close attention. And take notes! Any detail could be important.

Have fun on the mystery island!

Map

Each numbered circle is a place on the island. Each place is connected to others by paths. You can travel along the paths to get from one place to another.

You can't skip any steps along the way. If you have to go through **70** to get to **80**, for example, you have to solve the puzzle or make the right choice in **70**. To find out what happens in these places, you have to go to that section of the book.

You can't yet get to places with numbers in a dotted circle, like **90** or **110**, directly. You'll be told when you've unlocked access to them.

There are some mysterious places that are not shown on this map. You'll discover them on your adventure.

To begin your adventure, go to 1.

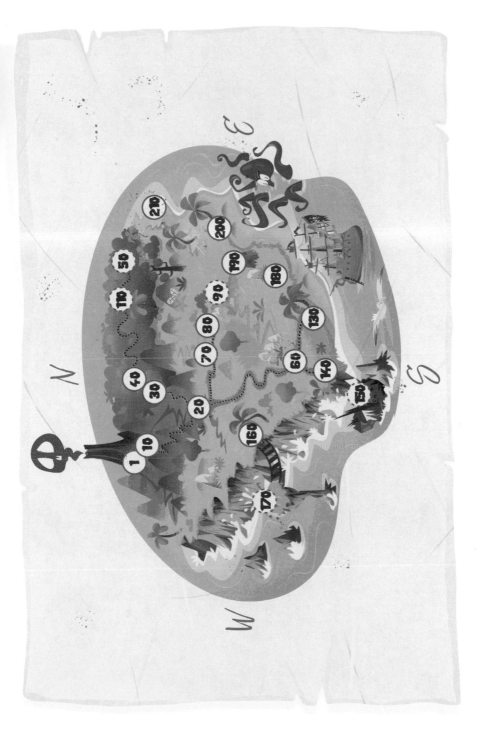

A Smoky Cave

"Cuckoo! Wake up, cuckoo! You can't stay here!"

Ouch! A parrot just bit your ear! That hurts! But it certainly wakes you up!

You get up, coughing. Your eyes sting when you open them. You're in a cave filled with a pungent smoke.

It looks like there was an accident, a cave-in. You have a really bad headache. You don't remember what you're doing here. You do recall being part of a pirate crew. You must have gotten knocked out by one of the falling stones. You get up slowly, in pain, but you're okay. Nothing's broken. You're standing. Behind you, the rear of the cave seems to be completely blocked by the collapse.

A parrot is flying around you. Not just any parrot! A beautiful macaw with red, yellow, and blue feathers.

"Cuckoo! I'm Harry, your parrot," he says. "Not to brag, but I saved your life. I was the one who told you to run away. The pirates you were with blew up the mountain! They opened up a hole for the volcano's lava. Whose bright idea was that?"

"What did they come for?"

"What are pirates always looking for, matey? Treasure!"

You pick up a **red scarf** on the ground and add it to your inventory. Make a note of this scarf in your inventory in **A3** at the end of the book.

To use it right away, like on your nose or your head, reference the table of combinations on the inside front cover or at the back of this book in **A2**. How does that work? You need to find the line for "Red Scarf" and look at what you can combine it with: your nose, your head, a rock, etc.

The numbers in the chart will show you where to go. Sometimes it will work out for you, sometimes not. Let's see whether you get it. Try the combination table with the scarf. Go to combinations on the inside front cover or at the back of the book. Read the result and come back here. You should try using the inside cover. It'll be easier.

Did you see how I just suggested using this scarf? You can also try using other objects you come across. To do that, just go look at the possible combinations.

The smoke grows even thicker and makes you cough even more. This smoke is dangerous. You know you can't stay here. How do you get out? To try to get through the stones, go to **2**. To search the cave, go to **6**.

 2

You move the stones around. Some are really heavy, and you have to use all your strength. You start to breathe harder because of the effort, and the acidic smoke goes deeper into your lungs.

Have you protected yourself from the smoke? If you haven't, you cough a lot. But since it's the beginning of the adventure and you're too young to die—even if it's just in a story—you can go back to **1** and make another choice.

If you have protected yourself from the smoke, you are eventually able to move a big stone out of the way. You create a small opening in the pile of stones—a way out of this cave.

Since you're little, you can slip through and get out. But before you do that, did you search the cave? You might find some tools that can help you on your journey. To search the cave before leaving, go to **6**. If you've already searched the cave, go to **10**.

3

You carefully wrap the scarf around a small rock. It's very cute. It looks like a tiny old lady with a scarf on her head. No, little pirate, be serious. Take your scarf back, go back to 1, and choose something else.

 4

You put the scarf over your nose and mouth. It filters a little smoke, so you can breathe better. What a good idea! Go back to 1, knowing you're now protected from the smoke.

 5

You wrap the scarf around your head and tie a knot. You really look like a pirate now! Well done! You have protected your head from the sun! Oh no. There's still that smoke. . . . Go back to 1 and try again.

If you haven't found a way to protect yourself from the smoke, you'll cough so much that you can't do anything, not even search the cave. You'll have to return immediately to 1. If you've protected yourself from the smoke, you can keep going.

While searching the cave, you find some **rope** on the ground. You wrap it carefully around your waist and add it to your inventory. Make a note of this rope in your list of objects. You can now combine it with other objects. For example, it might be long enough to help you cross a narrow river, or you could tie it and make a lasso. You'll figure it out! After all, you're a smart little pirate! Now that you've searched the cave, go to **2**.

 10

After crawling a few feet, you finally arrive at the mouth of the cave. Phew, fresh air! Freedom! You are on a small mountain overlooking an island. On one side, there is an idyllic landscape of beaches and palm trees. On the other, there's a thick jungle and a mountain trail that leads down to a rocky area and a pine forest.

Behind you, there's smoke coming from the top of the mountain. You quickly realize that it's a small volcano. This island must have sprung up from the ocean thanks to the volcano. And apparently, it's still active! You'd better keep moving!

You take the winding path down the volcano. Parts of the path are quite wide and easy, and other parts are steep and narrow—barely wide enough to walk through. In places, old lava flows have become crumbling gray rock.

Around a narrow bend, you discover a small **barrel of gunpowder.** Someone must have dropped it on the way up. It's still full, and the black powder inside is still dry. You pick it up. It might come in handy. Remember to make a note of it in your inventory. To keep going, go to **20.**

20

You arrive at the base of the volcano, to a flat area with some scattered trees. The main trail continues down to the sea. But you discover another trail, a smaller path leading to a narrow valley. There must also be a way to get to the jungle from here!

Where do you want to go? What do you want to do? Look at the paths available on your map on the inside back cover of this book. Remember, you need to unlock the places in dotted circles to get there. You can sometimes do that by using an item from your inventory (at the back of your book in **A3**) with another item or place by combining them using the combination tables in **A2.**

"I'm always full of ideas," Harry the parrot says. "So if you're stuck, you can ask me. Two heads are better than one!"

Let's go on an adventure! Look at the map and choose where you want to go!

To walk to the sea, go to **60**. To take the path to the narrow valley, go to **70**. To try to find a way toward the jungle, go to **30**.

You are surrounded by more and more trees, and the undergrowth thickens. The silence gives way to the sound of birdcalls and rustling animals in the brush.

Suddenly, a flock of multicolored birds takes flight. It makes you jump. You were just as scared as they were!

Harry is overjoyed. "Hey, those are my cousins!"

Sure enough, they are also macaws. The birds all have the same green on their heads, a bright yellow belly, and wings with blue feathers. It's an impressive sight.

Harry notices you and furrows his feathered brow. "What about me?"

You should know that parrots can be very jealous. When you don't play with them, they'll bite your ears!

"Yes, Harry, you're very handsome too with your red feathers!"

Along the way, you also find some delicious **fruit**. Add it to your inventory. The fruit is edible and very juicy.

If you keep going this way, you'll get lost in the jungle. If you think you have **something to help you find your way**, try a combination.

Otherwise, you keep going in circles in the jungle until

you end up finding the broken branches you stepped on earlier, and you return to the trail taking you back to **20**.

31

No, a lighter won't help you. You can see very well, so it's useless here. Fortunately, this tropical jungle is very humid. Otherwise, you could have started a fire!

Return to **30** and try something else.

32

You try to look through the bottle as if it were a telescope. But you're in the jungle, and you can't see beyond six feet with all the vegetation. Stop fooling around, matey!

Return to **30** and try something else.

33

I think it works better on your head. It'll protect you!

Return to **30** and try something else.

◎ 34 ◎

Of course that's what it's for! Thanks to this magnetic device, you can find your way in the jungle without getting lost. You can now use the small map of the jungle and its trails. You've unlocked access to a new place!

Well done! You can go to **40** to explore the jungle. But be careful—it's dangerous! It might be wise to return to the intersection of trails and to check out some other places first by going to **20**.

◎ 40 ◎

Warning! Do not keep reading unless you've figured out how to unlock access to this area. If you haven't, go back to where you were before.

Thanks to the compass, you can keep going. You enter the jungle, where there is no path.

You make your way between plants, trees, and vines. It's exhausting. The air is humid, and your skin quickly becomes sticky and sweaty. Insects buzz in your ears and bite you. And on top of that, you get the feeling you're being watched. Maybe some animal is sizing you up for lunch.

You try to get that idea out of your head, but you're very aware that you have no weapons to defend yourself with. It's dangerous out here. Just then, you notice distinct winding paths that you can follow, just like on the map. You can go from one numbered section to another since they're connected by a path.

Harry squawks. "Go around the island! Explore the entire island first!"

Have you explored everything? Do you have everything you need? Think carefully before you venture deeper into this jungle.

To take the path that goes south, go to **47**. To take the path that heads east, go to **43**. To head west, go to **41**. You can still return to the edge of the jungle, through **30**, and from there reach the trail crossing at **20**.

Your parrot perches on a branch. Then, gripping it with his claws, he spins around it again and again. What an acrobat!

"Do you have a sense of which direction you should go in?" he asks.

 41

This part of the jungle is full of flowers of all shapes and colors. It's beautiful! Maybe one of these flowers is the most useful. If you pick one, make a note of its color and check off **flower** in your inventory.

Be careful! Flowers can be poisonous! Don't pick them at random! From here you can go back to **40** or continue to **47**. You can consult your small jungle map at **40**.

 42

You look up, trying to see the sun so you can use it as a guide. Suddenly, you hear a rustling, and something shoots past you, barely missing you. How terrifying! You make out a scary masked face moving in the jungle undergrowth.

Is it an animal? A demon? It has arms. And a mask! It's not a monster but a human! He's a small, muscular boy, who has a blowgun ready to shoot. Then, suddenly, he screams, drops his blowgun, and grabs his foot. You take the chance to leap toward him. You see a little red snake with black markings scurry away. Careful!

The boy was bitten by a coral snake! He looks terrified. By his expression, you quickly understand that the snake in question must be venomous.

To help him, go to 100. To leave him here to his unfortunate fate, use your small jungle map to help you figure out where to go next.

43

You emerge at last from the thick jungle into a less dense, dark area. There seems to be some kind of wooden structure. Oh wait! It's not a fabricated structure; it's a gigantic tree! It would take several people to reach around it.

The trunk has many hiding places. You thrust your hand into one of them, but you pull it back immediately. It's covered in giant ants! You could get bitten. All you can do is go around the trunk and return to your jungle map and compass. To continue east, go to **44**. To go back north, go to **40**.

44

The jungle is dense, and you make slow progress. You stop to catch your breath and look up. You see an old canoe balanced in the canopy of nearby trees. It looks worm eaten. How did it get there? Did someone put it there? Was it caught up in a tropical storm and carried here by some horrible wind?

You try to climb the trees to get to it, but the bark is slippery. You quickly lose hope. Then you hear the rumble of the volcano. It's awe inspiring. You have to stay focused on your adventure so you can find Captain Flynn's darn treasure and convince your fellow pirates to leave this island before the volcano explodes! Go back to **40**, and be quick about it!

 45

The trail is marked with black stone posts with drawings of island animals carved into them. Despite the vegetation becoming overgrown again, you make good progress. You feel like you're getting closer to your goal. You're happily making your way down the trail when, suddenly, a stone underfoot gives way! Go to **120**.

Once you've made it out of your predicament, you can keep exploring by using the small jungle map.

 46

You walk through the vines and thorny plants. They haven't managed to slow your progress, but you feel like you're going round in circles. Luckily, you soon make out the shape of huts in the distance.

The huts are collapsed, half reclaimed by nature. You quickly understand that there was once a settlement here and it's now empty of inhabitants. All that's left is some pottery and rusty tools. None of it is useful to you.

To continue your journey and go south, go to **48**. To go east, go to **42**. To go west, go to **47**.

47

You emerge from the thick of the jungle into a clearing, where you soak in the sunlight. Then you see a dead pirate lying on a flat black stone! You shriek in horror! It doesn't look like he's been there for a very long time. You recognize Long John Silver by his wooden leg. He's a member of the crew, a pirate just like you! But he was a mean son of a gun who pushed you around and stole your rations when he'd had too much rum—you're just a cabin boy, after all. You're sad for him, but there's nothing you can do.

There is a dart sticking out of his chest. Pirates don't use darts. And he clearly didn't die of natural causes here on this stone. It's some kind of altar with engravings of animals. This island must not be deserted at all.

Looking closely, you see that the pirate is holding something tightly in his fist. When you pry it open, you understand why he was squeezing it so hard. It's an old **button** with a fleur-de-lis on it. It's a sailor's uniform **button**. The fleur-de-lis represents the kingdom of France.

You make a note of it in your inventory, in **A3** at the back of the book, and you slip it in your pocket. You can continue your journey by using the jungle map and your compass.

To take the trail that leads east, go to **42**. To go west from here, go to **41**. To go south, go to **46**. If you're scared and want to turn around, go back to **40**.

 48

Finally, and after an hour of trudging through the dense jungle, you find hope again. You hear cries of seagulls in the distance. Maybe you've finally made your way across this island! Excited and happy, you run toward the gulls. You push aside some leaves and find yourself at the top of a cliff. You see the bright blue ocean, a beach of fine sand, and, farther to the east, a smoking volcano. All this to get to a dead end . . .

It's so hard. You just have to turn around and go back to **46**.

 49

When you finally manage to get out of the thorny, sticky, and combative jungle, you encounter a black stone wall. You walk around it. You are standing in front of a small abandoned pre-Columbian temple.

"It's the end," says your parrot. What an ominous bird! Maybe he thinks it's almost the end of your adventure.

To take a closer look at the temple, go to **110**.

◎ 50 ◎

Warning! **Do not keep reading unless you've solved a puzzle to unlock access to this area. If you haven't, go back to where you were before.**

You find yourself in the darkness of the temple, with only the faint glow of the torch that you found and lit with your lighter. You shudder with excitement as you explore. You discover statues and an altar with offerings of dried and dusty fruit and flowers. This must be what remains of an ancient religion. There's nothing here that would interest a pirate in search of gold, gems, and other treasures . . . treasures like Captain Flynn's. The captain who tried to draw other pirates to the island so he could be rescued without risking a hanging from the navy. That captain who left his treasure here, who left the boy you met earlier to defend this temple.

And here you are at last, in the darkness of an ancient temple, so close to your goal. You see a heavy naval chest in a corner. It looks to be in great shape, still protecting the treasure inside. But it's much too heavy for you to move it alone. You'll have to open it. There are three locks on it. It looks like you have to insert specific objects in them.

What objects could help you here? Let's hope Flynn didn't take this secret to his grave!

Make sure you've explored every part of the island. Check your inventory and see whether you have three objects that once belonged to Flynn that might help you open the chest.

Harry pecks at your ear. Then he says, "Flynn's in his grave. Flynn's in his grave."

How sinister.

51

Using a key to open a chest seems like a logical thing to do! But that would be too easy. It turns only halfway. Flynn didn't lock his chest with something as simple as a key— even though that key was hard to get.

Go back to **50** and try again.

 52

There's a slot that could fit the ring, if you were to insert the top of it, the part with the skull and crossbones. You insert it, turn the ring, and hear a click! Harry hops around in excitement. You've unlocked the first lock!

If you've already unlocked all three locks, go to **59**. If you still haven't, return to **50** and keep at it.

53

You remove the cross you were keeping around your neck. The cord isn't going to help you, but the cross itself easily slides into the base of one of the locks. It's like a square key! You turn it using the arms of the cross and hear a click. You've unlocked the second lock!

If you've already unlocked all three locks, go to **59**. If you still haven't, return to **50** and keep at it.

 54

That's a practical object that you should always have around. And you found it near the captain's grave.

So it makes sense that you'd try to use it to get to his treasure. Unfortunately, it doesn't work. And you might want to take a closer look at those locks. There are three shapes for the keys: a square, a circle, and a cross.

Go back to **50** and try again.

55

Of course! The button has a fleur-de-lis, which was also on Flynn's gravestone. You insert the button into the lock with the round hole, and it disappears. Its shape seems to trigger some mechanism in the lock. You have unlocked one of the locks! Well done!

If you've already unlocked all three locks, go to **59**. If you still haven't, return to **50** and keep at it.

 56

Although the compass probably belonged to Flynn, it doesn't fit in any of the three locks.

Go back to **50** and try again.

Hooray! You've unlocked the three locks. You manage to open and lift the lid easily.

Your parrot is cackling and hopping around with excitement. "We won! We won!"

There is no gold in this chest. You are disappointed, but gold is heavy anyway. What you find instead are small bags of gemstones: emeralds, rubies, topaz. There is a different color for every taste. Best of all, they will satisfy your fellow pirates and convince them to leave this island!

You can go read the end of this adventure in the epilogue at the very back of the book! Congratulations!

⊚ 60 ⊚

Driven by the gentle slope, you quickly make your way down to a wide stretch of fine sand and scattered palm trees. What a beautiful beach! The ocean surrounds you. To the east, you see a group of pirates slumped at the foot of some palm trees. They are guarding a canoe and seem to be sleeping in the sun. In the distance, at sea, you see the ship that brought you here. Its black flag leaves you with little doubt.

Farther toward the south, it looks like there's a barrier reef nearby. You make out a dark mass in the white foam of the waves, not far from the shore.

To go talk to the pirates, go to **130**. To check out the dark mass, go to **140**.

⊚ 70 ⊚

The rocky valley continues alongside a ravine. You find a small stream of fresh water and take the opportunity to quench your thirst and wash the soot and sweat off of yourself. You hear a goat bleating in the distance. The valley continues to extend into a narrow ravine with a stream that's bordered by rocky ledges covered in pine needles. You could climb up the sides only if you were a mountain goat!

To keep going by leaping from one rock to another, go to **80**. If you decide you'd rather turn back, go to **20**.

 80

You arrive at the top of a 30-foot-high waterfall. The falling water sounds musical. It's very pleasant. The sun makes its way through the pines and creates a lovely rainbow effect on the splashing water below. You couldn't jump down it without breaking your neck. There's no tree you could tie a rope to. The boulders on either side of the waterfall create a big natural staircase. You climb down the first one. It doesn't move, and you don't slip. That's encouraging!

You notice then that the stone has an engraving. It says, "Do." Who carved that into the stone?

Then, looking closely, you see that each boulder has letters engraved. You raise your head and see a plank of wood hidden in a dead branch. It says, "Scale the rocks." Well, of course. How else would you get down? It's not like you'd jump.

Scale the rocks.

DO
TI
LA
DO
TI
RE
DO
TI

SO
FA
MI
TI
FA

On the next rock, you see "Ti" engraved. You easily make your way down to it. When you put your foot on it, it moves a little. How frightening! You move quickly past that one to the rock below. That one is engraved with the word "La." After that, you have to choose between two options. You can either jump across the water to reach the rock with "So" or continue your descent to the next rock, engraved with "Do."

The combination table (at the end of the book in **A2**) will show you where each rock will lead you.

Harry starts to sing. "It's easy to sing."

Yeah. So what?

"It's easy to sing while you scale the rock face."

Oh! Singing scales! What a smart bird!

81

That's a wide stone. It should be easy to land on. . . .

Aaaaaaaaaah! It moved! It wasn't stable at all!

You fall to the rocks way down below, breaking all your bones. Good thing this is just a game! Go back to **80** to try again.

82

You take a deep breath and go for it. You leap across the waterfall, getting a cool shower in the process, and you land on the rock on the other side. You made it! You are now on a boulder on the right side of the waterfall. You can easily go down to the "Fa" boulder below, or you can jump back to the other side to "Ti." It's up to you.

83

You make it down to the next boulder. You are on the right side of the waterfall. You can go across to go left on the boulder covered in moss with the word "Re" on it. You will have to jump! You can also lower yourself to the boulder "Ti" below you.

Think carefully, and go look at the combinations table at the back of the book in **A2** again.

 84

You have to jump to make it to that boulder. Let's hope you're right about this! You jump, getting a little wet on your way across, and land successfully. At least it's stable, and the moss isn't slippery.

You can continue down to the "Do" boulder by going to **89**, or you can jump back across to "Ti."

 85

You land on a slippery surface. Before you have the chance to regain your balance, you slip and fall.

You should pay attention to the order of the notes on these rocks. There is a logic to all this. Go back to **80** and try again.

 86

You miss the boulder and fall to the rocks below.

Go back to **80** and try again.

87

You land on the boulder without a problem.

The stone "Mi" is just below you and really easy to get to. If you don't trust it, you can jump to the other side of the waterfall, to "Ti."

 88

You miss the boulder and fall to the rocks below. Go back to **80** and try again.

89

You made it! Well done! You understood that you needed to sing the scale backward while scaling down the boulders.

Do-Ti-La-So-Fa-Mi-Re-Do. You take one last big step, and you arrive at the bottom. You've unlocked access to the next area! Go to **90**.

Warning! **Do not keep reading unless you've solved a puzzle to unlock access to this area. If you haven't and you used a map to get here, that's not fair play. Go back to where you were before.**

The ravine continues. The river gets wider, and it's more pleasant to walk along its bank. This area is shaded, sheltered by pines, with just the right amount of tropical sun. In the distance, you still hear the bleat of wild goats. Down in the valley, you soon see a hut. When you get closer, you make out some goats tied out front, some tools made of odds and ends, and a hammock between two trees. Someone has set up camp here!

"Hey! Is anyone in there?" you call out.

But you hear only the echo of your voice. If a castaway or an abandoned sailor lives here, he's either gone hunting or he's afraid of you.

A noise in the trees makes you turn around. A little monkey! It seems domesticated—it looks at you with mischief in its eyes.

"Hey there, little monkey," you call out to it. It stays out of reach.

You notice it's wearing a key around its neck. That's interesting. Maybe you have an object you can use to attract or catch it. Check out the possible combinations you can make!

Harry's feathers are standing on end. He hisses and bounces from one foot to the other. He's acting defensive. He's very jealous and doesn't like it when you pay attention to other animals. He just might nip you with his beak.

Afterward, you can retrace your steps, go back up along the waterfall, and take the trail out of the valley to the trail intersection by going to **20**.

91

Of course! You tie a lasso in the rope and throw it toward the monkey. He gets scared and rushes back up into the tree! That was a bad idea. You retrieve the rope. The monkey is watching you, curious.

Do you have another idea? Go back to **90** to try something else.

92

The monkey can't resist a treat. He comes down from the tree and reaches for the fruit. You give him a piece, and he eats greedily. Then you give him another, and yet another, urging him to come closer and closer.

As you prepare to catch him with the next piece, he jumps on your shoulder. He is so cute! And he trusts you. You give him the rest of the piece of fruit, and while he is eating, you look carefully at the key. It's a small **metal key**, like one that opens a sailor's chest. The monkey seems to like you. He's playing with your hair. You fool around with him for a while. While he's busy looking for lice on your head, you delicately remove the key. Make a note of it in your inventory. At that exact moment . . . go to **95**.

93

You open the barrel of gunpowder carefully and throw a little in the air. Nothing happens. Without fire, it won't burn. What a strange idea!

Think of a way to make this little monkey happy. Return to **90** to try again.

95

Just then, a shaggy-looking old man comes out of hiding. He's holding an ancient-looking musket. You don't know whether this pirate's gun is loaded, and you don't want to find out.

"Hello," you say timidly.

The old man only moans in response. He seems to be suspicious of you. You hand the monkey to him, and he nods. Then, using his hands, he tries to tell you that he lives here, hidden, and that you shouldn't tell the other pirates he's here. You realize the man is mute. Then he signals that you have to go to the wreck of his boat. He shows you a plank over the door of his cabin, where you can still read the words "*Fancy Pearl*." You understand that this is the boat that crashed into the reef a long time ago. The name reminds you of something else.

The old shipwrecked sailor gestures for you to leave now. You hesitate. He could come with you. You try to invite him to follow so that he can leave this island with you.

"No," he signs decisively. He seems to say he's too old for that, that he has lived happily here, and that he is afraid of other pirates.

You are sad to leave him, but your adventure must continue. To retrace your steps and follow his advice, go to **60**.

100

How can you help this boy? He stares at you with a mixture of fear and hope. Poor kid, he can't tell whether you're a friend or foe. What if you knew of an antidote for the snake venom? You have to figure out what that might be. *What are medicines made with?* you think. *Usually, they're made with plants.*

But you know nothing about the plants on this island. Which ones are poisonous? Which ones could help him? There must be information to help you with this somewhere.

When you've found the right plant, go to your combinations table (in **A2** at the back of the book) and test out its effect. If you're missing some elements, go back to **40** and explore other parts of the jungle. Act quickly!

Harry flits from branch to branch, pulls off a flower, and eats it. Will this parrot ever be of any use?

 101

You apply the flower to the boy's wound. He does not look reassured. The flower doesn't seem to have any effect. The boy gets weaker. . . .

Go back to **100** and try again.

 102

You make a poultice with the flower and apply it to his bite. The boy gives you an approving look and massages his foot. After a few minutes, the bite looks better! You've made yourself a new friend. As a sign of gratitude, he gives you a ring with a skull and crossbones on it. It's an old **pirate ring**.

You ask him where he got it. You realize that you can speak the same language when he tells you that his friend Captain Flynn gave it to him to protect his treasure. You wonder whether this boy knows where this treasure is. You explain that the greedy pirates you came here with won't leave without this treasure and that they are likely to find him and his family and hurt them.

A sad expression crosses his face. He says that he lost his family because of an illness. He tells you that he lives in the jungle alone with an old castaway named Roberts. He lives deep in a valley that's hard to get to, protected by a waterfall.

Flynn is dead and buried in his handsome French sailor uniform on Devil's Peak, facing the sea, as he said he wanted to be. He left cryptic clues everywhere pointing to his treasure! But, at the end of his life, the captain regretted sending so many bottles out to sea with maps pointing in the wrong direction, toward a cave on the side of the volcano. Flynn had said that, because of him, one day evil, lawless pirates would come here. This day has apparently arrived.

But all is not lost! You just have to find Flynn's real treasure! Go back to **42** and explore the jungle.

You apply the petals of the flowers that you picked on the boy's snake bite. He doesn't look very reassured. In fact, his condition gets worse.

Try looking for more clues instead of picking a flower at random. Go back to **100** and try again.

104

The large flowers that you've collected make a perfect poultice that's easy to apply to the wound. Unfortunately, he doesn't get any better.

Go back to **100** and try again.

105

These flowers are way too fragile. They fall apart in your hands and are useless. Harry suggests that you look harder than that before trying to heal the boy.

Go back to **100** and try again.

What a surprise! It looks like this could be the last trace of a long-lost population—perhaps distant cousins of the Mayans used to live here on this island after being driven away by the Aztecs and the Toltecs!

The temple is made from dark stone and has no visible door or stairs. How do you get in? On one side, there's an indentation that might hide a secret door. There's a big engraving of a bird on it. You see four deeper holes in it—one in the wing, one in its body, one in its crest, and there's also one in the eye that has a jet-black stone set in it. Then you see four other stones on the ground: one blue, one yellow, one green, and one red. When you pick them up, you notice that they all weigh different amounts. You have three places where you could put the stones and four stones. You probably have to do this in a very specific way, but how? Try using your combinations table at the back of the book in **A2**.

Harry lands on a branch and begins to smooth his feathers with his beak. He glances at you and says, "Oh, oh! It looks like my parrot cousins. Like the ones we saw earlier!"

111

You arrange the stones in a way that makes sense to you. Your parrot, Harry, is watching you, cocking his head skeptically.

Once you're done, you take a step back and admire your work. But nothing happens. Go back to 110 and try again.

112

You put the stones in their places: one at the top, one in the middle, and one at the bottom. It looks pretty. But that's all.

"It doesn't work! It doesn't work!" Harry mocks you.

Go back to 110 and try again.

113

You arrange the stones to match the plumage of the parrots you saw in the jungle: green for the crest, yellow for the body, and blue for the wings. Harry, your parrot, is flying happily around you.

Once you have put the last stone in place, you hear a hollow sound. The door begins to move slowly but surely to the right, revealing a passage into the temple.

You've unlocked access to a new place! Well done! To enter the temple, go to **50**.

114

You order the stones instinctively. Nothing happens.

How would the people who built this temple have done it? Go back to **110** and try again.

115

You place the colored stones using your intuition. Nothing happens.

Think of what the people who built this temple might have imagined. Go back to **110** and try again.

116

You arrange the colors to match those of your parrot, Harry. It's a lovely thought, but it doesn't work.

The people who built this temple didn't know Harry. They were probably thinking about other kinds of parrots. Go back to **110** and try again.

◎ 120

You fall into a pit. Fortunately for you, the bottom is not full of deadly spikes but is lined with an old pile of grass. Thanks to that, you didn't get hurt.

You get to your feet and try to climb out, but the sides of the pit have no footholds or handholds you can use. You fall back down into the pile of grass.

You've got to think quickly! On the right wall, there's some kind of stone dial. If you look closely, you can see it's got animal symbols on it. At the top, you see a kind of wave pattern that resembles water. In the center, you see a glyph that looks like an oval or possibly an egg.

What should you do? How can you align these symbols to help you get out of here?

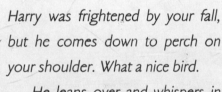

Harry was frightened by your fall, but he comes down to perch on your shoulder. What a nice bird.

He leans over and whispers in your ear, "You've got to get out of here, fast. None of this 'slow-and-steady tortoise wins the race' stuff. You don't have a shell to protect you when the volcano explodes."

121

You turn the dial to the left, and the fish lands between the two symbols with a click. Nothing happens. It was worth a try. But fish lay their eggs in the ocean.

Maybe another choice would work better. Go back to **120** and try again.

122

Should you turn the dial right or left? It doesn't make much difference. The dial turns easily, clicking as you pass each animal. Once you've got the frog in position, you wait awhile. Nothing happens. Maybe frogs lay their eggs in fresh water and not in the sea?

Go back to **120** and try again.

123

You turn the dial to the right and put this funny-looking creature on top. It's got a tail. Maybe it's a monkey? Apart from the device making a small click, nothing happens.

Go back to **120** and try again.

124

What comes out of eggs? Birds. You move the bird to the top of the dial. Apparently, it's not a seabird, because nothing happens.

Go back to **120** and try again.

125

Click, click, click. You turn the dial three spots, aligning the turtle with the other two symbols. And after a while, you hear a louder fourth click, and the bottom of the pit starts to rise, coming back to the level of the path.

You've made it out! You can keep exploring the jungle. Go back to **45** and choose a path from there.

126

You turn the dial left with conviction and align what appears to be a beast, maybe a cheetah, between the egg and the sea. Click, click. It makes no sense. Nothing happens.

Go back to **120** and try again.

127

An insect? A spider? What is this exactly? You're not sure. Whatever it is, it doesn't work.

You'd better think about this some more. Go back to 120 and try again.

130

As you approach, you make out four pirates. They are all asleep. There's an empty bottle of rum and open coconuts scattered around the beach. You pick up the **empty bottle** without thinking. You can add it to your inventory.

Suddenly, one of them wakes up and recognizes you! It all comes back to you: that's Henry, the second in command. He speaks in a weak voice, and his breath reeks.

"Arr! You little scalawag . . . what're you doin' here? You been out lookin' for that darn treasure for a looong time . . . up there on that volcano."

"Uh, the volcano began to rumble and smoke, so I ran." Your answer is probably not far from the truth as you shake with fear.

He laughs. "Why does this not surprise me? You always were a chicken! Well, do you at least know when we can get on our boat and leave? I've got a bad feelin' about this smoking island. The captain took off on his own and hasn't come back."

At the sound of this terrible name, one of the pirates wakes from his stupor and says, "Henry, don't you think it's strange that John Silver wasn't part of the volcano expedition? He's always the first to demand his share of gold, and he doesn't trust a soul."

"Well, that wooden leg of his is always givin' him trouble. He didn't want to climb up there."

You answer, an innocent expression on your face, "It sure is a steep climb! Hey, how about we leave now?"

"Ha ha! If you try to do that, I'll throw you overboard! We have orders to wait for the return of your expedition. And the crew won't go anywhere without their share of the treasure. We've all seen the treasure map from the bottle we found at sea. We ain't leavin' empty handed."

Well, at least you know now. You can't leave the island before finding the treasure. You eye the rowboat pulled ashore—the only way to reach the pirate ship anchored at sea.

Just then, an explosion reverberates throughout the island.

Both you and the pirates turn toward the mountain.

The volcano has woken up for real! A large plume of gray smoke is rising from the crater.

"If it were up to me, if it went off like that again, I'd leave," he says. "But orders are orders! Come on, boy! Try to make yourself useful. Go!"

You take advantage of the chance to get away. You can't get to the pirate ship yet. And if the rest of your expedition was killed during that landslide, you're not even close to being able to leave . . . unless the treasure is somewhere else and the pirates haven't found out how to get to it. They don't seem like the brightest crew. At least not any smarter than their cabin crew!

To go east on the beach, where there is a long stretch of white sand, go to **180**. To go west to the barrier reef, go to **140**.

◎ 140 ◎

You make your way over and between the rocks, climbing higher and higher. As you gain altitude, you make out an old galleon shipwrecked on a reef. It looks like it's been there for years. Time and storms have both taken their toll. The sea is raging off this part of the island, and to get there, you'd need to cross an inlet. But you can't swim very well, and the water's too rough for you. One of the masts is leaning a few feet above the turbulent water.

How can you reach it? This is a good time to use one of the objects you've collected. Check your inventory.

Otherwise, you can continue exploring along the coast by going to **160**.

Harry can fly. He doesn't care what you choose to do.

"Cuckoo, don't lose the thread!" He laughs. "Don't lose the thread! Don't lose the thread!"

What a bird.

141

You throw a piece of fruit at the wreck. It falls into the sea and attracts a giant bird, who then quickly loses interest. Oh well, you have more.

Return to **140** to try something else.

142

You pick up a round stone, wrap the rope around twice, and tie a tight knot. Then you throw that stone as hard as you can toward the mast, holding the other end of the rope in your hand. The rope unfurls, and the stone goes past the mast. Then gravity takes hold, and, as it falls, the rope wraps itself around the mast. You pull on it, and it holds tight. All you have to do is tie the other end of the rope around yourself and you'll be ready to get across to the wreck. Go to **150**.

143

You consider throwing the bottle against the hull, as though you were christening the boat. It's a nice gesture, but it won't help you reach the wreck.

Return to **140** to try something else.

144

You could blow everything up! You could combine the lighter and the gunpowder, but you'd still have to reach the wreck somehow. A barrel of gunpowder and a lighter won't create a bridge for you! Come on. Think harder!

Return to **140** and try something else.

Warning! **Do not keep reading unless you've figured how to unlock access to this area. If you haven't, go back to where you were before.**

The outside of the wreck is in bad shape—algae and barnacles cover the wooden hull. Clearly, someone used a bunch of the wood before you got here, because planks seem to have been carefully removed, leaving gaping holes in it. It looks like ribs of a sleeping giant. The captain's quarters and the entire back of the boat are still in relatively good condition. You can still make out the name of the ship: *Fancy Pearl.*

You arrive at the door of the captain's cabin, but it's closed. Maybe you have something you could open it with.

Harry gets upset and flies around the wreck. "Monkey! He has the key! The monkey!"

*If you don't have anything you can use to open the door, you might want to return to **140** and explore the island some more.*

151

You take the pendant from your pocket and try to get it into the lock. It doesn't work. This was not a good idea.

Go back to **150** to try something else.

152

Of course! The monkey's key! It unlocks the door easily. Open it and go to **155**.

153

You pour a little gunpowder into the lock to blow it up! Ingenious, but you don't have anything to light it with!

Go back to **150** to try something else.

154

You pour a little gunpowder into the lock, then you carefully approach with your lighter. The powder ignites immediately, and you burn yourself a little. You quickly move away. The lock explodes, and the door is weakened. You give it a big kick, and it's open! You can go in the cabin by going to **155**.

155

 You enter what must have been Captain Flynn's cabin. While searching, you find a logbook. The captain has recorded his story. You can go read the captain's log at the back of the book in **A1**. It must be teeming with useful information about the island. Reading this will not be a waste of time!

After you've read the log, go back the way you came, returning to the beach by going to **140**.

160

The beach narrows, and you find yourself wedged between a tall cliff and a narrow strip of rocky shore with waves crashing against it. You climb up some boulders to the top of the shore and follow the ridgeline. Beneath you, the beach has disappeared, and the waves are breaking against the cliff. You see what must be walruses or sea lions down below.

You turn a corner and see a rocky pinnacle jutting out of the ocean. It has a flat summit, and leading to it is a wooden bridge, swaying in the wind. You arrive at the bridge and look down. There is a long drop to the rough sea below.

You clearly see a group of stones arranged on the other side. It's worth investigating, but you must cross this bridge to get there. Some of the planks are worn and seem like they are about to break. It looks like these are planks taken from the hull of the wreck.

Look at the bridge; you may find clues to help you.

Harry flies over to the other side. He doesn't need a bridge. But as he sees that you don't follow him, he comes back and perches on the two stones in front of you.

"What are you waiting for? What are you waiting for?"

That's when you see the clue! How clever!

Your turn! Which planks are you going to step on?

Look closely at the bridge and the two stones at your feet. You can only reach the first three planks on your first step. And you'll have to jump to get to that third one! Worst-case scenario, you can use the ropes to make sure you don't fall.

Go right to the number of the plank you want to step on first. To step on the first plank, go to **161**. To take a big step to land on the second step, go to **162**. Or you can jump to the third one by going to **163**.

161

You put your foot on the nearest plank and just begin to shift your weight onto it when you feel it crack in two. You barely have enough time to throw yourself back.

Go back to **160** to try again.

162

You put your foot on a plank that looks worm eaten, but it holds. You can continue.

Now you can move to the next one by going to **163**, take a big step onto the one after that by going to **164**, or bravely jump to the third plank ahead of you by going to **165**. Take some time to consider your options!

163

You land on the plank, and it cracks immediately. You hold tight to the ropes so you don't fall. The bridge keeps swaying more and more. This is hard!

Go back to **160** to try again.

164

You land on the plank, and it immediately cracks in two. You can't stop yourself from falling through the bridge. This is the end of your adventure.

But since you're still an inexperienced young pirate, you can go back to **160** to try again, if you want. Be sure to look at the hints in the image!

165

You take a deep breath, jump, and land safely on the plank. Keep going! You're almost there.

To step on the next plank, go to **166**. To go to the one after that, go to **167**. To jump to the third plank, go to **168**.

 166

The board creaks underfoot. You manage to save yourself only because you are holding the ropes tight!

Go back to **165** and try again.

 167

You step forward confidently and . . . it holds! Either you've got the hang of this or you're very lucky! You're almost there!

To make one last jump, go to **170**. To proceed with a little more caution and walk slowly, go to **168**. To go to the plank in between these, go to **169**.

 168

You land on the plank, and it immediately cracks in two. You can't stop yourself from falling through the bridge. This is the end of your adventure.

But since you're still an inexperienced young pirate, you can go back to **160** to try again, if you want. Be sure to look at the hints in the image!

◎ 169 ◎

You jump and fly to the next plank . . . and fall through it. It's all over for you.

Since you're still an inexperienced young pirate, you can either start the book again or go back to **160**. Be sure to keep an eye out for hints!

◎ 170 ◎

Warning! Do not keep reading unless you've solved a puzzle to unlock access to this area. If you haven't and you used a map to get here, that's not fair play. Go back to where you were before.

On Top of Devil's Peak

Well done! You got to the other side! This is no small feat!

The top of the landform is very impressive. You can see out to sea for miles! But you still have space to walk around without getting too close to the edge.

There is an old pile of wood and branches with black marks. There must have been a fire here used to signal boats. Beside it, you find an old flint **lighter**. It still works, which means you can make a fire or light a flammable object with it.

There's also a small pile of stones that would be hard to miss. It's a grave! The inscription says:

Captain Flynn
French sailor

Pirate at heart

With faith in God

My treasure will not
follow me to my grave

That seems like a clear epitaph. Is there any hidden meaning to this inscription? Did Captain Flynn want to convey a message? It's a mystery! Retrace your steps and go to **150**. Have you gone to all the places you can so far? If you've figured out how to visit the wreck and made it into its cabin, you've explored this side of the island! Don't forget that you have a map.

180

You look around at the huge white beach with scattered palm trees swaying in the wind. Masses of small crabs are tossed about by the waves. You pick up a couple of **crabs** easily. This scenery would be heavenly if vacations had been invented and you had a round-trip ticket. But getting out of here is not going to be that easy. You can continue to explore the island by going to **190**. You can return to the pirates by going to **130**.

 190

The beach gets narrower and narrower. You end up on a cape with a stone and wooden fort that looks like it was built a long time ago. Maybe it's a relic of Spanish conquistadores? Who knows.

Facing the ocean, you find a wooden board that a desperate artist engraved with the directions to known ports: Seville, Spain; Port Royal, Jamaica; etc. A compass rose indicating north and a compass are attached to it. You pull the **compass** off of the board. It's going to come in handy!

At the base of the fort, among the stones, you notice something sparkle in the water. Is it a jewel? You can step over the ruins of a wall and go look by going to **200**. You can continue to a distant cove by going to **210**. Or you can return to the beach with the crabs by going to **180**.

200

The boulders along the waterfront become crumbling stones as you make your way along the cape. This side of the cape is calm, sheltered from the wind, with only a few small waves disturbing the surface of the water. You can clearly see a pendant shining beneath the surface, half buried in the sand. Is it a cross?

Suddenly, you sense movement. The sand becomes cloudy, and long arms covered in suckers emerge! It's an octopus! You jump back, fear fluttering in your stomach. The animal looks at you with strange eyes. It looks more curious than aggressive. It won't eat you. But if you want to dive in and get the cross, you'll need more than courage. You'll have to find a way to distract the octopus! Check your inventory to see what you can use.

Harry plays with a small shelled nut. He seems to be looking for food inside. He holds the shell with a foot and lifts it to his beak. He finds the nut inside and eats it. Then he says, "Yo ho ho and a bottle of rum!"

It's amazing what animals can do when it comes to food!

201

You approach the edge of the water and throw the flower in toward the octopus. It retracts one of its arms and seems indifferent. The flower floats there for a while until a wave carries it away.

Go back to **200** to try something else.

202

The octopus jumps on the poor crab and cracks it open in a flash. It has eight arms, so it all happens very fast! You only manage to dive in before it finishes eating it. It spits a cloud of black ink at you, and the cross disappears. You get scared and climb out of the water quickly. You were so close!

Go back to **200** to try something else.

203

You grab a small crab and put it in the bottle. That's going to give the octopus a hard time! You fill the bottle with seawater so that it will sink, cork it, and toss it toward the octopus. The bottle doesn't even make it to the bottom before the octopus grabs it with one arm

and probes the cork with another. It seems to quickly understand that the crab is trapped in the bottle, but it uses its eight arms to continue to explore other options. It's an intelligent creature—it'll figure it out. While it's trying to solve that puzzle, you dive into the water in search of the pendant. It's hard to see with all that sand floating around. Can you see it? When you find it, make a note of the **cross pendant** in your inventory.

Go back to the wooden fort at **190**, or continue on to the cove at **210**.

204

You might as well give it a try! You tie the rope in a noose and try to catch the octopus. You try dangling the rope to distract it. But you can't get close enough, and the octopus doesn't give it the time of day.

Go back to **200** to try something else.

210

You continue past the cape and see a cove with white sand and clear blue water. . . . It would almost be repetitive if it weren't so beautiful, so calm, so peaceful. . . . Wait!

A turtle just came out of the water! It's a light tan and brown animal covered in spots and with big black eyes. Adorable! The Caribbean turtle goes farther up the beach, to the foot of palm trees on the edge of the jungle, and buries her eggs in the sand. Soon, these eggs will hatch, and the small turtles will have to reach the sea quickly if they don't want to be devoured by predators. It's the eternal cycle of life.

You have almost made your way around to the other side of the island. But then you come to an impenetrable mangrove where the jungle meets the ocean, and you have to turn around. To return to the fort on the cape, go back to **190**. If you've already explored everything on this part of the island and you want to check out the other side, go to **140**. If you want to return to the trail crossing, go to **20**.

 220

That's great—you get the idea! By coming here, you would see what happens when you use the rope.

Return to the beginning of the book.

 221

Well done! You've figured out how to combine objects!

You can now go back to the beginning of the book.

 222

There is no grappling hook in this adventure, and you don't see it in the inventory, but you get the idea.

Go back to the beginning of the book.

A1—Captain's Log

Year of grace 1680. I am Captain Flynn. This is the logbook of the Fancy Pearl, my ship.

On a night of a fierce storm, we crashed on the reef of an unknown island. Only Roberts and I survived, because we know how to swim. We were able to cross the stretch of sea separating us from land.

Once the sea calmed down, we collected some food, a musket, and some rum bottles from the wreckage. We established camp near a stream, hidden in the bottom of a valley.

I am afraid we are not alone on this island. I have often felt as though we are being watched.

§

We drank half the rum. I want to send distress messages in the empty bottles. I'm torn between my desire to be rescued from this island and the fear of being arrested for piracy. If we're rescued by pirates, like us, they will surely steal my treasure. On the other hand, if the Spanish or the English rescue us, we're as good as dead.

§

The island is not deserted. A tribe of natives lives in the jungle. We were quickly discovered and surrounded.

Fortunately, they are not hostile. Communication is not easy, but we have managed to get on their good side.

My treasure does not interest them!

§

The natives have shown us healing plants and taught us where to find food. The island is full of animals and food sources, but beware of the snakes.

Some are venomous. They are recognizable by their colors and their ringlike patterns. I wrote everything down in this log so as not to forget this information. There is more in the next chapter on animals.

§

I've come up with a way to get us out of here. I drew a fake treasure map, which points to a wrong place! The pirates who will follow it will climb the volcano. Thirsty for their wealth, they'll neglect to search the rest of the island. This will leave us, me and Roberts, with the help of the natives, all the time we need to seize their ship and escape. With my treasure, I will be able to convince the crew aboard to join my cause. I know pirates well. They are interested only in profit.

§

Roberts, my companion in misfortune, has taken a liking to this island. I think he likes life here more than the life of a pirate. It's simple and quiet, mostly hunting and gathering. Here we have plenty to eat, and we are at peace. I'm bored, so I try to learn from the natives.

They taught me to heal with plants. Their knowledge of the flora of the island is impressive. They showed me a small temple buried in the jungle that conceals fascinating secrets. It's protected by hidden mechanisms. Everything here has its own logic!

§

The natives have fallen ill. It's terrible. I don't know what to do to help them. They are not familiar with the disease afflicting them. Perhaps we brought it with us.

I am wracked with guilt.

I'm desperate. I am seriously ill too. Only Roberts and a young boy have not fallen ill. I will not write in this journal where I hid my treasure. I will take it with me to my grave. . . . No. I'm delirious. The fever is getting to me! Nobody will come for us. All is lost

Island Animals

This island is full of fascinating animals. The jungle is home to a species of multicolored parrots—yellow, green, and blue.

The monkeys are intelligent and curious creatures that can be won over with fruit.

The cape is home to octopuses. They are very fond of shellfish and crustaceans. They grow larger to survive, at the expense of their numbers. The smaller ones don't survive.

The wide beach is full of edible crabs. You can catch them with your bare hands. This is fortunate, because fishing is difficult due to strong currents and wind. We risk getting pulled away from the island and lost at sea.

Both the monkeys and natives harvest coconuts. It's a convenient way to hydrate. Once they are cut open, the interior contains a very nourishing liquid.

The jungle has two kinds of snakes: some are venomous and very dangerous; others are harmless.

Fortunately, the natives have described a flower that can save anyone bitten, provided it's applied directly to the wound.

Island Flowers

Description of the Flower	Color	Use
Six heart-shaped petals	Blue	Brings down ███ fever
Four petals	Yellow	Upset stomach
Bell-shaped chalices	Pur███	████████████
Nine separate petals	███████	Snake bite
Five round and pointed petals	Bl███	███████ache
Four flame-shaped petals	Red	Wounds, infections

A2—Combinations

With these tables, you can try out your ideas. You can combine one object with another. For example, you could open a chest with a key. You can even combine an object with a place.

	Head	Mouth or Nose	Rock
Red Scarf	5	4	3

	Empty Bottle	Lighter	Compass	Red Scarf
Jungle	32	31	34	33

Waterfall

Do	Re	Mi	Fa	So	La	Ti
85	84	83	87	82	80	81

	Barrel of Gunpowder	Rope	Fruit
Monkey	93	91	92

	Barrel of Gunpowder & Lighter	Rope	Empty Bottle	Fruit
Wreck or Shipwreck Mast	144	142	143	141

	Cross Pendant	Barrel of Gunpowder	Metal Key	Barrel of Gunpowder & Lighter
Door to the Captain's Cabin	151	153	152	154

	Flower	Crab	Crab & Empty Bottle	Rope
Octopus	201	202	203	204

Antidote

	Red	Orange	Yellow	Blue	Purple
Flower	101	102	103	104	105

Temple Stones Puzzle

	Crest	Wing	Body	Go to
Color	Yellow	Green	Red	111
Color	Blue	Green	Yellow	112
Color	Green	Blue	Yellow	113
Color	Yellow	Blue	Green	114
Color	Red	Blue	Green	115
Color	Green	Red	Blue	116

Chest

Pirate Ring	Metal Key	Cross Pendant	Lighter	Compass	Button
52	51	53	54	56	55

A3—Inventory

☐ Red scarf

☐ Rope

☐ Barrel of gunpowder

☐ Compass

☐ Fruit

☐ Cross pendant

☐ Flower

☐ Metal key

☐ Pirate ring

☐ Lighter

☐ Empty bottle and its cork

☐ Crab

☐ Button

EPILOGUE

The ground starts to move, and an intense rumbling shakes the temple walls! The volcano! You had almost forgotten about it in the excitement of finding the treasure. Judging by the rubble falling all around you, it's time to run. You grab as many gemstone bags as you can and tie them around your neck by using their long drawstrings. Harry is panicking. His feathers are bristling as he whistles frantically. You've got to get out of there quickly!

You make your way out of the temple and into the humid jungle. The boy is there. He seems healed.

"I'm going to help you," he says. "You have to leave this island and take those pirates with you!"

"And you?" you ask. "Are you going to die here in the eruption?"

"This is my island! My people have lived here for generations. I'm not afraid of the volcano."

He guides you through the jungle. He shows you shortcuts that you never would have found on your own. You run with him through the leaves, jumping over streams, using vines.

In less than five minutes, you are near the beach where the pirates and quartermaster are waiting. They're staring at the black smoke emerging from the volcano with worried looks on their faces. They can't see you. You're still hidden in the brush alongside the beach.

"Put on your most terrified expression and run to them," the boy says. "Beg them to leave right away. I'll scare them by using my blowgun. You only have to say that you are being pursued by a hostile tribe, and they will believe you."

"Goodbye. Thank you for your help."

"Thank you for saving my life! I attacked you, yet you helped me."

"You couldn't have known I wasn't bad. So many pirates are greedy and bloodthirsty."

"You're not like that. You've made good choices. Now leave!"

You take a deep breath, get up, and run out of the brush, screaming. "I found it! I found the treasure!"

The pirates look stunned. It's definitely a strange sight.

You throw them one bag, then another, and you open the contents of a third. There is greed and hunger in their eyes.

"Where did you find that, boy? Where are the others?"

"In the volcano's cave! The earthquake made everything collapse! I was only able to escape because I'm so small. . . ."

"How strange. Wasn't there gold? No silver coins or ingots? Would you lie to us? Show us the way there."

Oh no! If you take them to the volcano, you'll never make it out alive, and they'll figure out that you're lying. And if you admit to lying and bring them to the treasure chest, they might find your friend or Roberts . . .

Just then, a dart lands in the sand right next to you.

You yell even louder, "Natives! The island is inhabited by cruel natives! They've already killed Long John Silver. I saw it when I was making my way back through the jungle. We have to go now!"

Just then, a second dart shoots out of the brush and pierces a pirate's hat. That convinces them. You hear frightening growls come from the tree line. This seals the deal. The pirates believe they're being attacked. They don't look any further. They put the boat in the water and jump in with the bags. You don't ask for your share. You just jump on board. You are finally leaving this island.

They row at full speed toward the ship. As you're pulling away, the volcano explodes! You see rocks fall on the mountain and in the nearby jungle.

A huge cloud of smoke follows, then lava. It runs down the cliff and into the sea, where it makes a sound like hot metal plunged in water! You reach the pirate ship just in time because it was already setting sail!

Everyone gets on board, hoisted by the pirates on the ship, who are curious to know what happened!

Everyone is more than ready to leave. They are afraid of the eruption, and they have the treasure! They are already talking about how to split the loot.

The pirate ship sails away from the island, and the volcano continues to erupt. Through the telescope, you see that the lava is flowing right into the sea. The volcano that created this island is now enlarging it. In truth, there's very little danger for your friend and Roberts. They can live on the beach on the other side of the island for a few days during the eruption.

You think you see a silhouette on the beach watching. Yes . . . it's that good old Roberts with his musket in his hand. The boy is beside him, holding his blowgun.

Your fellow pirates are singing to their good fortune.

One of them comes to see you. "Hey, boy, how's about you tell us of your adventure? You were mighty brave to escape the volcano and those natives! Spill the beans!"

Will you be able to tell the true story someday? You who found so much more than Captain Flynn's treasure, you who also learned the power of compassion, kindness, and intelligence.